Courageous Ali
and the
Heartless King

By Tariq Mehmood

Illustrated by Abbas Shah

Courageous Ali
and
The Heartless King

Published 2006 by Satchel
All rights reserved
admin@satchel.info

Printed by LPPS Limited,
128 Northampton Rd, Wellingborough, NN8 3PJ

The Beggar

The beggar came out of the blazing sunlight and stopped outside the shade of a banyan tree. The hood of his tattered brown cloak covered his face and a tall wooden staff shook in his leathery hand. He stared at a group of children who stood under the canopy of the tree.

'Ali! Where are you?' The call of an anxious mother cut through the silence.

The beggar lowered his head and stepped back.

The children scampered, shouting, 'Beggar! Beggar! Beggar!'

The beggar moved into the shade and leaned his staff against the trunk of the tree. He took a clay bowl from inside his cloak, placed it on the ground, and sat

opposite it with his head bowed. Closing his eyes, he listened to the cooing of a dove somewhere above the dangling roots of the banyan tree, calling ceaselessly for its beloved. He had no idea how long he sat there listening to the dove. Time had no meaning for him now, but when he opened his eyes he saw a woman coming towards him. She held a small cloth across her face with one hand and with the other a young boy by the arm. The boy carried a black water pitcher which he tipped towards the beggar and said, 'Drink.'

 'I do not deserve such a generous gift,' the beggar said, without lifting his head.

 'Tell me old man,' the woman asked gently, 'you must have seen much and been to many places. I am a simple woman and my son Ali is all I have. He has not seen his father, Jamal ur Rahman, for many years. Each night he wakes up crying for him.'

The beggar lowered his head even further. The dove went silent. 'I may have come across him, but would not know who he was...' the beggar replied sorrowfully.

'Come now, old man,' the woman interrupted. 'Drink some water before you die of thirst.'

'I must earn my drink. I am forbidden to accept a gift for free.'

'Why?' the little boy asked.

'That is a long story,' the beggar replied.

'What is it that you do?' said the little boy.

'I am a storyteller.'

'Then tell my son a story that will chase his nightmares away,' the woman said, squatting opposite the beggar.

The beggar lifted his head and through the ripped hood looked at the woman's dark eyes. They were filled with grief. He raised his shaking hand and waved it through the air before beginning to speak. As the words rolled out of his hood, other children came in ones and twos and sat around him in a semi-circle.

'The story I will tell you,' the beggar began, 'is the tale of a brave young boy who, like your beautiful son, madam, was also called Ali. The Ali in my story, like this lovely Ali, also lost his brave father, when he was only ten years old.'

Paupers and Palaces

Not long ago, this land was ruled by a terrible king called Khauf. He was a selfish man, who built massive palaces for his own pleasure and cared not what happened outside their walls. Everyone lived in dread of him, his spies were everywhere and people talked in whispers. It was forbidden to walk with raised heads.

Even though Khauf's kingdom produced half the milk in all the world, children went hungry. All the milk was taken by Khauf and woe betide anyone who dared keep a few drops for themselves.

It was early in the morning on the first day of the new moon. It was the time everyone hated, the time when great urns had to be filled with milk and left outside people's houses, from where they were collected by soldiers and taken to the palace of King Khauf.

'Just take one bottle for Aisha, father, how will Khauf know so little is missing?' Ali pleaded, pointing towards his poorly sister.

Ali's father looked across at his mother. She shook her head. Nevertheless, he scooped a few cupfuls of milk out of the urn, put them into a jug, and hid the jug under a bed.

'Evil rules and hungry spies are everywhere,' the mother warned. 'They have special ways of seeing, even from above the clouds, and they know how much milk our cow will give even before we milk it. God willing we will get through.'

'I am tired of getting through,' the father said, wiping sweat off his forehead. 'Our children go hungry even when they are sick.'

That day, when the soldiers came to take the milk from Ali's house, they measured the urns, but it was as though they already knew. They turned the house upside down until they found the hidden milk, and Ali's father was dragged away.

From that day onwards, Ali cried for his father every night. On his thirteenth birthday he asked his mother, 'Why should that Khauf take all our milk? It is ours. Why should he take my father? He should be here with us.'

'You talk too much like him, Ali,' the mother warned.

'At least he had courage,' Ali replied, holding back his frustration.

'And he is dead.'

'Have you seen his body, mother? Have you been to his grave? Do you even know where it is?' Ali knew he was hurting his mother.

'No one ever comes back from Khauf's dungeons,' his mother replied, rocking Ali's sister.

'I will not live in fear of death and die every day,' Ali protested. 'I will live only to end this evil.'

It was the time of day when the soldiers came for their collections. 'Take this milk outside,' the mother said, putting Aisha down gently. 'You need wisdom as well as courage.'

Holding an urn by its two handles, Ali walked towards the patchwork of wood and twigs that passed for a door and pushed the urn outside onto the street. Bored soldiers stood at regular intervals. Workers were going from house to house, collecting urns full of milk which they placed onto carts. There were two workers to each cart. They lifted a full urn, put it neatly on its side, then returned an empty one in its

9

place.

While the workers had their backs turned to the cart, Ali checked to see if any soldiers were watching, but they seemed to be half-asleep. He jumped onto the cart and hid behind the urns. The cart joined a long line of others rattling along to the end

of the city, towards the Great Palace of King Khauf.

Through a crack in the side of the cart, Ali watched the faces of the children whose hungry eyes stared at the milk going by. From each street more carts joined the line. Soldiers stood on guard. When Ali's cart crossed the bridge he saw the huge archway to Khauf's palace with its fearful warning: *Anyone entering without permission will be turned to stone*. Statues of people who it was said had been turned to stone stood in neat rows along the road. Some had faces filled with terror, while others covered their faces with their hands. Ali searched for his father, but could not see him. Each cart was checked by sentries as it approached the gate. A dog jumped in and out of carts at random, wagging its tail. A tall guard patted its back, dropped a morsel of food into its mouth, then placed a collar around its neck. As Ali's cart drew nearer, he held his breath, keeping a wary eye on the dog.

The guard moved towards Ali's cart, stopped, pointed to something behind the palace doors, and ordered, 'The next twenty five carts over there!'

The dog growled. The guard pulled its leash tighter and snapped, 'Their Majesties cannot be kept waiting all day.'

Ali's cart pulled into the palace, turned down a pebbled road, and disappeared into a tree-lined avenue. His cart, followed by twenty-four others, made its way deeper and deeper into the palace grounds. Apart from the hooves of the mules, clomping on the pebbled path, everything was eerily silent.

The path led into a gigantic warehouse. Endless lines of storage tanks were stacked on top of one another. New urns were taken from the carts, arranged into straight lines, and their lids removed. A great clamp picked up the urns one by one and placed them onto a belt which transported them towards a leather flap, through which they disappeared. A line of empty urns clanged its way back along another belt.

Ali waited until he was well in shadow, slipped out of the cart, and hid behind a line of urns.

The Spitting Royal Brothers

Over the clanging of the urns, Ali could hear the sound of singing and laughter. Pushing his head through the leather flap, he gazed into a magnificent room. Every inch was painted in the most wonderful colours he had ever seen. He could hardly believe his eyes. Milk gushed down a funnel into a large tank from which it flowed down carved horns into two smaller tanks at opposite ends of a gigantic pool. It poured out of two golden taps, one in the shape of a swan and the other an elephant, falling in unbroken arcs into the pool. Incense smoke rose all around. A soft wind blew through the silk curtains that descended from the tall ceilings.

Two men were prancing around in the

pool. A third was sitting at a table a short distance away, his head buried in a table piled high with books. Ali inched forward for a better view. There was no mistake. King Khauf, with his short curly hair and his thick moustache, was hard to miss. Ali had grown up under the shadow of Khauf's statues. Khauf's portraits were everywhere. Every classroom in every school had his picture, sometimes carrying a sword, sometimes looking serenely into the distance, but more often beaming a fatherly smile. Even if you hated him, you had to put a smiling picture of King Khauf centre stage in your house. He's nothing like the strong young man in the statues, thought Ali. He has a little pot belly and that moustache is grey!

King Khauf sat near the swan tap, pushing his toes up and down in the milky bubbles. His beady eyes were fixed on

King Gosler who lay at the elephant end of the pool, staring at the ceiling, opening his mouth like a fish. Ali looked in disbelief at King Gosler and wondered what the most powerful king in the world was doing here. Ali had imagined someone as mighty as Gosler would have a deep, thoughtful, perhaps kind face. But King Gosler had over-sized pointed ears that drooped like those of a donkey, and he was dribbling like an idiot.

King Gosler sat up abruptly and the forefinger of his right hand disappeared into his right nostril, taking with it a tuft of overgrown nasal hair. He swivelled his finger around, then pulled it out. It brought with it an elasticised bogie which twanged around his finger. After examining the bogie from different angles, King Gosler flicked it to the other end of the room and watched its flight as it twisted towards

Prince Sticker. The bogie stuck to a silver goblet and slithered onto the table.

Looking at the two kings, Prince Sticker lifted his head and smiled broadly. Though Ali was hidden behind the urns, he felt the evil eyes of Sticker scanning him. He knows I'm here, Ali thought nervously.

Prince Sticker smoothed his long black coat, straightened his starched shirt collar, and continued to stare in the direction of Ali before returning to his books.

King Khauf dived into the pool and emerged a moment later close to King Gosler's feet saying, 'Oh Majesty of Majesties, you who have blessed me by coming to my kingdom, on this, Mother of All Occasions, let me at least clean the hair of your nose.' Before he had a chance to reply, Khauf pulled on Gosler's nasal hair. Gosler immediately sneezed covering Khauf's face with a right royal dollop of green, slimy phlegm. Khauf continued without wiping his face, 'There, there. Oh Sire of Sires and Lord of Lords, all bogies are out and all sticky stuff off.'

King Gosler tried to move away from Khauf and slipped. His foot came out of the milk. As King Gosler steadied himself, Khauf knelt down and licked King Gosler's foot. 'Your Gracious Kindness, if you don't think it too impudent of me, I have been thinking, maybe you could give me but a little minute to make a small request.'

King Gosler twitched his ears and Khauf added quickly, 'Oh King of Kings, allow me, your loyal servant, to say, don't you think it is now time to let my kingdom trade with everybody else? I mean, I will, of course, always honour and respect everything you say, but the trouble nowadays, Your Majesty, is this. I am worried about the people of my kingdom. My subjects, the ungrateful scumbags, are getting a bit restless with all these restrictions. Some of them have the audacity to complain that they can't get any medicines and their children are hungry. But I do sometimes worry that things like this could lead them, one day, to rebel against me. And if they do this sort of a thing here, it could spread, and who knows where it might end.'

King Gosler twitched his nose and Khauf said dejectedly, 'Perhaps Sire would like to think matters over for a while?'

Prince Sticker jabbed a piercing stare at Khauf. Avoiding Sticker's eyes, Khauf twiddled his stubby thumbs nervously. King Gosler floated around the pool again, quacking like a duck.

Sticker sniggered, then beckoned Khauf towards him with the long index finger of his right hand. 'Come.'

Stepping out of the bath, Khauf brushed

his hairy arms and reluctantly went towards Sticker, mumbling, 'You come to my country as my guest, Prince Sticker, and you insult me by calling me over as you would a dog.'

'You are too sensitive, Khauf,' Prince Sticker laughed. 'If I thought of you like that, I would have whistled.'

'Oh, that's OK then,' Khauf giggled. 'It is just a misunderstanding.'

'King Khauf is fond of misunderstandings!' Prince Sticker thundered, slapping the table loudly.

'Yes. Yes. We have lots of them, don't we?'

Khauf doubled over with false laughter. Milk dripped off him, making a small pool close to his big hairy toes.

'This is no laughing matter,' Prince Sticker said angrily.

'You don't understand the understandings we have with His Majesty Gosler,' Khauf said, wiping tears from his face. 'No one understands an understanding as well as one that is understood by us.'

'Understand this, you moron,' Prince Sticker said, jabbing his finger into Khauf's breast where half of it disappeared into the grey curls of Khauf's chest hair. 'You are not taking enough milk from your subjects.'

'Don't tell me how to run my own country. No-one like you tells Khauf how to run his affairs.'

'You can't be as stupid as they say - surely you know which foot the boot is on?' Prince Sticker asked.

'I am not wearing any boots,' Khauf retorted.

'You are truly idiotic,' Sticker smiled, 'or else you are pulling my leg.'

'I never touched you,' Khauf said, nodding towards the pool, 'and if you insult me again, especially in my own palace, then I will tell my good friend King Gosler.'

'As you wish, Your Majesty,' Sticker smirked. 'Please do not disturb your relaxation.'

King Gosler continued floating around in the milk. Seeing Khauf enter the pool, he tapped his nose, opened his mouth, and then, turning his head towards Khauf, said excitedly, 'Me first!'

Khauf smiled, and nodded in readiness to start the game.

King Gosler and Khauf scooped mouthfuls of milk and, in turn, spat jet streams as far as they could. From where he was hiding, Ali saw King Khauf take out his famous shining teeth. Khauf pulled his cheeks in and then fired a jet of milk which King Gosler found impossible to match. After the third go, King Khauf started jumping up and down, his knees almost touching his chest, shouting, 'I win! I win! I win!'

'Cheat! Cheat! Cheat!' King Gosler stomped madly around the pool.

'I must go and tell Dir and Dur,' King Khauf said to himself, excitedly jumping out of the pool.

The mention of Dir and Dur sent a shiver down Ali's spine. These were King Khauf's special dogs which, it was said, were the only creatures he confided in. Ali turned to look at where Khauf was going, then froze, terrified. Someone was looking straight at him. Then he relaxed. The round-faced boy with unkempt curly black hair was his own reflection. The mirror magnified the freckles on his face.

Turning away from the mirror, Ali heard Prince Sticker shouting to Gosler.

'He is not paying dues on millions of gallons,' Prince Sticker said, pointing to the record books with a bony finger. A smile stretched across his angular face, showing a gleaming set of teeth. The smile seemed to be stuck. Pushing the chair back, he stood up, put a foot on the chair, tapped his needle fingers on the table, and said, 'And this is why. Here is his little secret.'

King Gosler's eyebrows lifted to the top of his forehead. He opened his eyes so wide Ali thought they were going to fall out of their sockets. Pulling impatiently on his nasal hair, King Gosler clucked like a brooding hen, then chuckled, 'Cheat? Me? Oh no. No, never. No one. No.'

Prince Sticker stared as King Gosler punched the milk in frustration then shouted across to him, 'He isn't just cheating in spit fights. Sire, if you come over here, I will show you. He really has a big secret.'

Scratching the top of his head, King Gosler skipped over to the tall figure of

Prince Sticker. Nothing really made any sense to King Gosler. He could not understand figures at the best of times.

'That disgusting thief has been developing a secret weapon,' Prince Sticker said, tapping a finger on his chin. 'A deadly secret weapon.'

'A weapon of deadly secrets,' squeaked King Gosler.

'More secret than any secret weapon and more deadly than any deadly weapon. Here, Sire, it is plain to see.'

'More secret than any secret and more deadly than the deadliest of secrets and more deadly than any deadly weapon,' King Gosler said, looking over the books.

'I heard stories from my spies, but I had no proof before,' Prince Sticker added. 'It is the Daddy of All Weapons.'

'I hope it is not a grandaddy...' King Gosler squeaked.

'It is worse than that, sire. Much, much worse.'

'That Khauf is a menace to me!' King Gosler said, folding his arms across his chest.

'He is a menace to humanity, Sire,' said Prince Sticker with a widening smile. 'He could take over the world. It is surely a matter for the Court.'

'Yes. Yes. To the Court.'

Khauf and Ali Meet

By the time Khauf returned with Dir and Dur, King Gosler and Prince Sticker had left by another entrance. The dogs looked like mirror images of each other in their shining black skins. They had short ears and enormous mouths and it was said they could even bite through cement. Khauf tied the dogs' leashes to a metal ring nailed into a pillar. The dogs immediately

scented something and pulled towards Ali. Realising that the dogs were tied, Ali took a deep breath and stood up.

The dogs snapped at Ali, rage flashing in their eyes. The sound of their barking reverberated around the room.

'Who are you?' thundered Khauf.

'I am Ali, the son of Omani the farmer,' Ali replied, clenching his fists. 'Your soldiers took my father. I want him back.'

'There are thousands of Omanis. And how dare you question me, you insolent little brat. I will feed you to my dogs.' Khauf clapped his hands, 'Guards!' But the barking of the dogs drowned his words.

'You are not the God of your statues,' Ali laughed. 'I saw the way you behaved towards those foreigners.'

'I am your God,' Khauf thundered, pointing towards the dogs. 'Dir, Dur, get him. Guards!'

The dogs pulled furiously at their leashes. Ali saw the metal ring inching out of the pillar. He turned and ran. The dogs broke free and rushed towards him. Ali dived through the flaps, running frantically between the columns of urns.

Escape from the Palace

Ali squatted in a dark corner watching the urns of milk stream into the warehouse. The barking of the dogs was getting louder. He crawled backwards, then tensed as he felt someone's breath on his neck. A hand clasped itself across his mouth. 'Ssshh.'

Ali turned his head. There was just enough light for him to see. It was a boy, about the same age as himself.

Taking his hand off Ali's mouth, the boy pointed to a large urn, saying, 'Quickly, in there. Those hounds are on your scent.' Handing Ali a thin pipe, he added, 'Use this to breathe.'

Milk gushed over the rim as Ali disappeared into the urn. A hooter boomed. There was a noise like a log being dragged across the floor and the urn began to shake. He heard the sound of marching feet. Someone shouted a command and the marching stopped. Judging from the commotion, soldiers were spreading out across the warehouse, looking for him. Someone was rattling the urns, the rattling getting louder each time. He held his breath. A hoarse-voiced man shouted another command. The warehouse went silent. Then Dir and Dur began to bark.

Opening his eyes inside, he expected to see a clear milky world, but it was dark and murky. A hazy light strained down from the top. He heard the dull vibration of people walking by. The light seemed to be getting brighter. Taking a deep breath, Ali pulled the pipe into the milk as a screeching noise came from above him. He looked up again.

It was definitely brighter now, as though someone was shining a ray of light into the mouth of the urn. They can't get my scent now, thought Ali.

Sticking the end of the pipe out of the milk every so often, Ali breathed as quietly as he could until he heard the horn again. He felt a hand on his head. Lifting his head from the urn, he saw it was the boy. Ali looked into the boy's blue eyes. There was something strange in those eyes.

'Why did you risk your life to help me?' Ali asked, as he climbed out of the urn.

'My name is Waheed. I have been here for two years,' said the boy, adjusting his cloth cap. 'My father is the keeper of the ancient secrets. King Khauf's men came to our village, accusing us of keeping milk. They took the first twenty people they came across and made them work in the palace in exchange. My father was at work in the ancient city at the time. I have not met him since that day.'

'You have been here two years!' Ali exclaimed. 'Have you not tried to escape?'

'Everyone is so scared of King Khauf,' Waheed replied. 'People here do not believe they can do anything. Besides, if anyone tries to escape, King Khauf orders their whole family to be executed.'

'What of your father?'

'He has taught me to be patient,' Waheed answered. 'I have been waiting for the right moment to escape.'

'When will that be?' Ali asked, wondering if he would have to stay here for two years.

'I cannot escape on my own, for should I die in the attempt, I will take all the secrets I have learnt with me,' Waheed said, pointing to a packet hidden beneath his shirt. 'In here I have three hairs, from each of the kings. I managed to get Khauf's hair without much problem. He moults like his dogs. But the other two, well, who knew they were going to be here, and it took longer.'

'What are you going to do with their hair?' asked Ali.

'My father will use these to find out their weaknesses so they can be destroyed.'

'I will not stay in this place for a moment longer than I have to,' Ali insisted.

'Yes, because of you, all my plans could be spoilt. The guards are looking for you.'

'I had to find out what Khauf did with our milk.'

'And what are you going to do with this knowledge?' asked Waheed. 'You cannot leave here on your own. No one has ever done this.'

'I managed to get in,' Ali replied, 'and we will find a way out.'

Waheed smiled.

'My name is Ali,' said Ali. 'I am the son of the farmer, Omani. Our house is by the bridge near the date trees on the bank of the river. My father was also taken by Khauf's soldiers. Maybe he has been turned to stone, but I could not see his statue out there.'

'No one comes back from the dungeons,' said Waheed sorrowfully. 'We only see the statues.'

'There is trouble brewing in our land,' Ali warned. 'I heard it with my own ears.'

'There is always trouble here,' Waheed replied, scooping up a fistful of milk from a passing urn, 'and this is the cause.'

Someone whistled. Waheed pulled Ali behind an urn. They sat until someone whistled again, then stood and walked to the door. It groaned as Waheed pushed it open and stepped into an alley.

The alley ran between the warehouse

and a high outer wall. There were countless doorless rooms, cut into the outer wall. Nodding to the nearest room Waheed said softly, 'This is where the mules are kept. Many of these rooms have passages linking one with the other. We can hide among the animals till the new moon.'

'What a disgusting smell,' said Ali, walking into the room.

A mule pursed its lips.

'Enjoy it, you only have three days of it,' Waheed replied, from deeper inside.

Dogs barked from outside.

As his eyes adjusted to the darkness, Ali saw Waheed standing near a hole in the side of a wall. A grey mule passed its tired eyes over Ali as he made his way towards Waheed. The dog's barking was getting louder.

Squeezing Ali's hand, Waheed

whispered, 'God will find a way to keep the dogs off our scent.'

'What's that?' Ali asked, snatching his hand from Waheed.

Waheed heard it too. He bent down and wriggled through the hole in the wall. Ali followed him. The next room was much bigger, with an arched doorway that led into a larger chamber. Drums were beating outside the palace walls and trumpets were blowing. Streaks of light came through the decaying plaster. Ali peeped through the cracks and jumped back in fright. 'King Gosler and Prince Sticker,' he whispered.

'Don't worry, they can't see us,' Waheed assured him.

Ali looked out again. King Gosler and Prince Sticker were leaving. Gosler was fast asleep in his carriage. A nervous Khauf offered his hand to Prince Sticker, but Sticker brushed the hand away, flicked his cloak across his shoulders, and stepped into the carriage without even a farewell glance at Khauf. Ali watched as the carriage sped away. He wondered why they were leaving in such a hurry.

What Ali didn't know was that, even before coming here, King Gosler had ordered the convening of the Court of Peace. He had summoned all the kings and queens of the world.

The Court of Peace

The Court of Peace met in a fabulous blue chamber with a painted glass ceiling and white marble walls. Two enormous blue curtains hung behind a stage with a podium for honoured speakers. Two red carpets, made of the purest of silks, were laid out in front of rows of chairs on which kings and queens had been waiting for many hours. Some threw paper balls at each other, some pulled faces, while the fattest ones doubled up and slept, snoring loudly.

When Gosler entered the chamber, drums and trumpeters burst into life and the assembled leaders stood. The court applauded as King Gosler, followed by Prince Sticker and a host of advisers, ascended the podium.

As the applause died down, a group of soldiers dragged an enormous object onto the stage. It was as tall as two men and as long as four, and covered in a thick blue cloth.

King Gosler tapped the table, his dribbling nose twitching. Then, wiping his nose with the back of his hand, he announced: 'Kings, Queens, Leaders of the World, we all know that horrible horriblists and their fathers' fathers are all horriblists.' Gosler stopped, bent over, and started flapping his arms and clucking like a hen. Then, licking his lips, he proceeded to neigh like a horse.

The audience waited expectantly for a translation. Prince Sticker stepped forward. He could speak fluent Chicken and was a master of Horse-speak. 'His Majesty King Gosler says: The world is confronted by a menace the like of which has never been seen before. Today this honourable Court is faced with its greatest challenge. Evil men are planning terrifying deeds. But they will be stopped and King Gosler is hungry for Freedom's march. So hungry, he could eat a horse and chase the jockey. My king will forever hold the torch of Freedom. We will shine Freedom's light everywhere, in every dark corner of the world. We must act now. There is no room for complacency. We must act together and not count the chickens before the rooster's laid the hen.'

Prince Sticker paused. The Court held its breath. Drums rolled. King Gosler raised his arms like a wrestler, jumped up, and punched the air.

As the drums faded, Prince Sticker said, 'Our wise king wants this honourable Court to stand up and be counted. It should stand up to these horriblists. It should become relevant or it will become irrelevant.'

Prince Sticker paused. King Gosler pulled on his ears, stuck out his tongue, and wiggled his nose, saying, 'That Khauf, Evil. Me, Good.'

Prince Sticker resumed his translation: 'Khauf's devilish deeds are already in front of this honourable gathering. His evil mind does not care for the goodness King Gosler has shown him. You are all aware of how he has disregarded the decrees of this Court. We have our special inspectors checking on his compliance, but they have been thwarted at every turn. Recently, King Gosler and I took a trip in person to see Khauf, to try to resolve the issues between us. And what did we discover?'

King Gosler wiped his forehead with a dirty handkerchief. It slipped and fell to the floor. When he looked up, he mumbled, trancelike, 'Freedom's Freedom. Blood of son. More bloody Freedom.'

Again Prince Sticker stepped in. 'King Gosler says he has a message from God Himself. The right thing must be done. This matter cannot be ignored any more. He has seen irrefutable evidence of Khauf's secret plan to conquer the world.'

Folding his arms across his chest, King Gosler patted his behind and let out a loud, 'Yahoo,' before saying, 'Bad man. Secret secrets. Kick buttocks.'

Prince Sticker nodded politely to King

Gosler and addressed the court, lowering his voice to a sinister whisper. 'Khauf has gone from bad habits to being habitually bad. He has been funding a secret programme to develop a deadly weapon… a secret army of camels. And these are no ordinary camels.'

The Court descended into pin drop silence as the Prince turned to the object on the stage. Prince Sticker pulled a wand from his pocket and with a few clicks that echoed throughout the hall, extended the wand into a long stick that tapered into a point. He tapped on the draped object. Drums rolled as the cover began to slide off. The drums stopped beating. A laser ray fell, illuminating a model of a camel with a devilish face. Two razor sharp fangs glistened from its open mouth. Its eyes were deepest red and its face was turned towards the chamber.

A yell of terror cut through the silence of the chamber.

The Prince pointed to the camel's backside and pronounced slowly and clearly, 'This is what Khauf's camels look like.' He paused before adding, 'They can fart to command.'

The Court let out a resounding, 'Fart to command!'

Prince Sticker continued. 'They can poo to command.'

'Poo to command!' the Court said in unison.

'And they can burp to command.'

'Burp to command!'

'Lords and Ladies, Kings and Queens of this world,' Prince Sticker continued, 'Nothing could prepare us for what we discovered next. These secret camels have other secrets.' He turned towards the camel, pointing to it with his stick. Something began to pop out of its backside, slowly revealing itself to be a white balloon. 'When they fart, they let out a mushroom cloud which gets bigger and bigger and bigger. The smell is worse than that of rotten eggs, worse even than rotten

apples. It is a cross between vomit and dirty socks! These clouds can destroy everything for miles around, even entire countries.'

The Prince popped the balloon with the end of his wand and tapped on the camel's behind again. A large round object dropped to the floor. To cries of astonishment, the Prince continued: 'And the poo of these camels is the size of footballs. It is no ordinary poo! It surely is the grand-daddy of all poos! It is the most dangerous poo ever to have been done by anything at anytime in the world. Not only does it smell of a dirty camel's backside, but just one lump could destroy us all. He already has thousands of tons of this camel stuff, and we know exactly where all his-'

'Khauf's kingdom is very big,' someone interrupted. 'How can you be so sure?'

The Prince looked over to King Gosler, who scratched his head and burped.

'There are knowns and known unknowns,' Prince Sticker replied, after a thoughtful pause. 'We know all the knowns, and we will get to know the unknowns as soon as we know them. Until then we do know that they are all in the north, south, east or west. '

The assembly applauded and cheered. The Prince spoke again as the noise in the chamber died down, 'He has also created a special unit called the Holy Camels. These can fly and could reach here within forty-five minutes and poo all over this chamber...and we would be no more.'

The chamber went silent.

'Prince Sticker, please explain to this Court,' a voice asked. 'His Majesty King Gosler has not suggested these camels have wings. Nor can we see any on the beast behind you. Now we know you need wings to fly. So how can these camels possibly fly? And if they can indeed fly, then can they poo whilst flying, and if so how do they ensure they poo on their intended target, or do they stop in order to take aim?'

Prince Sticker thought for a while and answered, 'That sir is a very good technical question, but His Majesty is not a technician and neither, for that matter, am I.'

Turning towards the camel again, he tapped its head with the stick. The camel's mouth opened, followed by a loud burp. The Prince looked around. Four figures covered from head to foot in white cloth ran onto the stage.

'We have uncovered one more dastardly ability of these camels. When they burp, they let out tiny little germs. If you come into contact with even one of these, you will feel very sick. Your skin will turn yellow. Your eyes will roll. You will get cramps in your stomach and uncontrollable diarrhoea. Death will take place within a few hours. The only way to approach a burping camel is to be covered from head to toe in a white suit.'

Many members of the Court held their hands across their mouths in shock. King Gosler punched the table a few times and then slumped into his chair. Prince Sticker carried on: 'These camels are not born like normal camels. They are bred in secret mobile sheds. But these camels need to drink lots of milk, and this is why that rascal Khauf has been deceiving us. We have no choice. We must stop this evil man. Either he must voluntarily disarm or we must disarm him. This man must be brought to justice or justice taken to him.'

The last words of Prince Sticker echoed around the chamber. King Gosler started to clap, and Prince Sticker joined him, smiling as broadly as ever. Slowly, everyone in the hall began to clap until a lone voice screamed out, 'Let King Khauf have a say!'

For a moment, everyone stopped

clapping.

King Gosler croaked in anger.

'You are either with us or against us,' shouted Prince Sticker. 'This Court must be relevant in this world or become a relic of the past. We must find the camels and destroy them.'

The assembly started to chant:

'Down with farty camels!'

'No to pooey Camels!'

'Down, down, burpy Camels!'

Prince Sticker smiled a knowing smile. What the assembly didn't know was that, at the same time as summoning the Court of Peace, King Gosler had ordered the full mobilisation of his army. Even as the Court debated, the King's soldiers, like an endless stream of ants, began to march out to far away places. The attack on Khauf would begin on the next full moon.

The Field of Statues

Ali and Waheed stayed hidden amongst the mules for three days, leaving only once when thirst forced them to sneak into the warehouse to gulp handfuls of milk before returning to their hiding place. They knew that the next evening, the evening when Khauf's soldiers would leave the palace to collect milk, was their only chance of escape

That time swiftly arrived.

It was the night of the full moon. Hundred of carts, full of empty urns, stood in columns. Ali and Waheed sneaked into the storeroom and hid themselves inside urns in one of the carts. They waited for the palace gates to open, but when at last the car began to move forward, Ali heard dogs barking and soldiers shouting orders. He sat as still as possible, trying not to breathe.

He heard someone tapping the urn beside the one he was crouching in. Then the shadow of a soldier blotted out all light.

Ali jumped out as fast as he could and rolled several empty urns on top of the soldier. The soldier stumbled and fell. One urn rolled past Ali and stopped by a statue of a man with outstretched arms. Ali quickly crawled across the road and hid by the base of the statue. He watched Waheed pull himself out of the urn he had been hiding in and run towards Ali.

Two guards headed towards the noise. Ali heard one of them cursing, 'They just don't stack them properly like they did in the old days.'

Ali and Waheed crawled a distance away from the road. They hid by a statue of a man whose arm lay shattered on the ground. Ali felt deeply sorry for the man. Even if he was brought back to life, he would always be without an arm.

They found themselves in a field of statues of men and women of all shapes and sizes. There were thousands of them, all along the perimeter wall and way down to the banks of the river. Some of the gaps in the otherwise symmetrical lines of statues were filled with cactus plants, each with beautiful, brightly coloured flowers protruding from their thick arms.

Filling his lungs with fresh air, Ali said, 'Well, we haven't been turned to stone.'

Enjoying the scent of the flowers, Waheed did not respond at first. Then suddenly he tensed.

A soldier was watching over the workers who were putting the final touches to a stone statue. 'Hurry now,' the soldier was saying. 'You don't have all day.'

'I should have known,' Ali whispered. 'Everything about Khauf is false.'

'Maybe, just maybe, my father is alive,' Ali thought, keeping a sharp eye on the soldier. The soldier eventually led the workers back to the palace.

They would have waited a few more moments, but the terrifying barking of Dir and Dur resounded from the palace. The beasts were at the gate in no time, frothing at the mouth. They sniffed the ground and raced towards Ali and Waheed. Throwing caution to the wind, the two of them ran towards the river at the bottom of the hill. Ali slipped. The dogs were almost on him. He felt the dog's breath on his foot, then he began to slide down the steep bank. He fell flying into the river.

Ali screwed his eyes tightly shut as he went down. He heard the water gushing below and then felt its cold embrace.

Opening his eyes, Ali saw fish swimming calmly around him. 'We made it,' he thought. Then he saw Waheed struggling in some reeds. The current was pulling him below the surface. He was in danger. Bravely Ali swam towards him and pulled at the weeds. But he couldn't free him. Ali dived down and bit into the reeds, gnawing with all his might to free his friend. At last, he felt the reeds begin to tear. He ripped the remaining ones away with his hands. Waheed floated back to the surface and, after coughing the water out of his lungs, grinned in gratitude. Together they swam downstream.

Ali had grown up on the banks of this river and when he began to see the familiar sights of his childhood, he knew they were out of danger. There, he and Waheed pulled themselves out of the water. He saw

the two smooth rocks where his mother used to chat with the other women as they washed clothes. No-one was there, only three leaning date trees, shading the pool. Ali smiled as he thought how he had learnt to swim in the shallow pool by the side of the rocks, how he used to cover himself head to toe in mud, then wait for it to dry and flake before jumping into the pool. His mind was awash with things he wanted to tell his mother. Maybe he could still find his father. How many other people like Waheed were around? Maybe they could all join together and find a way of saving some milk for the little children.

Out of the water, Waheed turned his back to Ali and adjusted his clothes. Then together they clambered up the bank. Reaching the top, Ali stared in stunned silence. Almost every house had its windows blown out. Some had roofs missing and stood like half-broken statues. Dust clouds hung over the houses and a pungent smell clung to the air.

Frantically, Ali ran down the street. The once bustling bazaar was empty. Turning the corner, Ali stopped. A dog was looking at him sorrowfully and, behind the dog, a woman was doubled over, holding the small body of a child and rocking her from side to side. Where previously there had been a row of houses, there was now a giant crater. At the edge of the crater, what was left of Ali's house stood smouldering.

'Allah!' Ali screamed, and then recognised his sister.

The Graveyard of a Million Children

The graveyard was a lush green place, sheltered from the desert winds by two rocky hills. It was almost a city, lined with trees where whatever was planted took root. All manner of song birds had built their nests in the trees. Each time a new child was brought in, these birds went silent, then after the funeral, as the parents and loved ones were leaving, they sang a deep lament. Though this song was filled with sorrow, it helped all who brought their children there to find some peace. Many of the children had died from hunger, others had fallen ill, never to recover, and hundreds had died in the way of Ali's sister, Aisha.

'Something came out of a clear blue sky,'

his mother told him. 'At first there was a buzzing sound, as though a fly was trapped, but then the buzzing got louder and louder until it became a roar. The roar got louder and louder. Then everything went silent. There was a flash of light, followed by a loud bang. The ground shook as in an earthquake and the air caught fire. That is when your sister breathed her last.'

The evening sun was setting as the heat of the day was chased by cool evening winds. Ali and Waheed had walked to the graveyard with Ali's mother. Mother and son now sat beside Aisha's grave. 'Who is that stranger over there?' Ali's mother asked, wiping her tears after finishing her story. 'He was sitting close to our house when you arrived, and now he is here. Maybe he is one of Khauf's spies.'

Ali looked around for Waheed. Like the stranger, he was nowhere to be seen. Walking away from his sister's grave, Ali said, 'Mother, I care not for Khauf's spells or spies. I will destroy him or die trying.'

Placing a hand on Ali's head and the other on her chest, his mother said, 'As surely as I brought you into this world and fed you the milk from my breast, I wish to see no other mother go through what I have. I bless you with the milk of my breast.' She bent down and picked up a pinch of earth. Rubbing it into her son's head, she said, 'I bless you with this earth. Everything below and above it is yours. Go, rid this land of evil.'

While his mother talked, Ali kept an eye on the stranger, then realised it was no stranger at all. It was a discarded old robe. The fading light had been playing tricks with his mother's eyes. The candles flickered around them. People drifted away. The birds began singing in wondrous harmony, as the lowering sun left faint crimson streaks across the skyline. The intoxicating fragrance of queen-of-the-night rose up from the bushes, mingling with the rich scents of jasmine and roses.

'Come back to me on your wedding day,' Ali's mother was saying, when there was a sudden gust of wind. Ali turned. The old robe was speeding towards him, tossing and turning in the wind. As Ali tensed, the robe rushed closer then lifted itself off the ground and floated over his head. As it did so, Ali thought he saw a pair of eyes shinning down at him. He felt he had seen them somewhere else.

Suddenly, the birds stopped singing and the ground began to shake. The candles along the path flickered violently, and something screeched across the sky before the graveyard was filled with a deafening bang. Everything was covered with smoke. When the smoke cleared all Ali could see was the empty path leading deep into the cemetery. It had been torn in two by a smouldering crater.

'Come on, Ali, we have to get out of here,' Waheed said, jumping out from behind a bush. 'Wake up, Ali!'

Ali blinked his eyes and, pursing his lips, nodded to Waheed. Yellow and blue flames were racing across the sky. Some flew towards King Khauf's palace, others towards the city. Ali looked for his mother but could not see her. He began to call for her, but Waheed shook him by the shoulders and shouted, 'Ali, we have to leave now.'

'My mother…' said Ali, but Waheed had grabbed his hand and was leading him along the path that veered to the left, snaking around graves and towards the hills.

As they began to climb, a long object with an arrow-like wing buzzed over them. A ferocious jet of blue light gushed from its rear. The object lifted as it got closer to the next hill then turned away to the right until it became a small dot. After a few moments, Ali heard a tremendous bang.

The hill around him started to shed stones which rolled noisily downwards. The land past the hill was engulfed in flames. Many miles away, Ali could see faint lights moving towards them.

'It has begun,' he heard Waheed say.

Ali turned around. But Waheed was nowhere to be seen.

'Waheed, why do you hide from me?' Ali asked apprehensively.

Waheed stepped out of the shadow of a tree, accompanied by an old man. Ali tensed, then picked up a rock and took aim at the stranger.

'What will your puny rock do against the monsters in the sky?' the stranger said, stepping forward. The rock dropped from Ali's hand. 'And to think my daughter thought you were the right one!'

The stranger put his arm around Waheed's shoulders.

'Your daughter?' Ali exclaimed, stepping backwards.

'Yes, my daughter Waheeda. We must move now,' Waheeda's father said turning towards a large tree. 'It is the end of Khauf but the beginning of a new nightmare for us.'

The Well of Ancient Knowledge

At first Ali was shocked at the thought of Waheed being Waheeda, but then he began to smile. He was still smiling to himself when he realised that Waheeda and her father had begun to climb a jagged rock face and were moving very quickly. Ali rushed to catch up with them. Waheeda stopped by a thick bush as her father disappeared beneath it, effortlessly twisting his body as she held the branches back for him.

When Ali reached the bush, Waheeda grabbed his hand and led him beneath. Ali found himself inside a tunnel which widened into a damp cave. Water dripped all around them as they walked deeper and deeper inside. Soon they could see the flames of torches coming towards them, shadows bouncing off the walls. 'There is nothing to fear,' said Waheeda.

'I'm not scared,' Ali lied.

'There is nothing wrong with being scared,' Waheeda replied, turning to look Ali in the eye. Her face was shining in the light of the flames. 'From here we go by boat.'

For the first time, Ali noticed two men standing in a boat in a river snaking around the bottom of the cave. They were dressed in rags, identical to Waheeda's father, who was already sitting between them. Reflections of the torches trembled in the silky water. Waheeda took Ali's hand, and led him into the boat. The man at the front pushed the boat away with a long pole while the other began to paddle with a large oar.

Together, they manoeuvred on the river

as it flowed through the mountain, fighting to stop the boat smashing against the rocks.

The river twisted and turned in the palm of the jagged insides of the mountain. The world beyond the light of the torches was blanketed in darkness. They passed through a cave that burst into life as hundreds of bats whizzed around them. The torches fluttered furiously in the wind. Using all their strength, the men slowed the boat to a crawl. The walls were now so close that Ali could run his hand across their damp, rocky surfaces.

'Get down,' shouted Waheeda's father.

Everyone squatted and held on tightly to the sides of the boat. The boat inched forward, passed under a low ceiling and emerged on the other side in a wide cavern. A beam of light caught two waterways meeting. A small waterfall fell near to the merging rivers.

The boat slowly drifted past overhanging rust-coloured mossy rocks that seemed to have been carved into long thin beams.

The men brought the boat to a stop. They walked up a rocky path towards a glow in the distance. Ali followed, wondering what it could be. He smiled when he saw moonlight flooding into the cave. The men looked to Waheeda's father, who had pushed off his hood. He had straight silvery hair, and his eyes gleamed in his wrinkled face.

Waheeda held her father's hand. Her father pointed towards the light. 'That path leads to the city of the ancients,' he said, taking a deep breath. 'Never has the air smelt of pain as it does tonight, nor have the stars been blotted out by so many flames. Now, my children, you have travelled long, and there is much for you to learn. But first you must rest. We are safe here.'

Carrying a torch in her hand, Waheeda led Ali towards to a small room carved into the side of the cave. Straw had been spread across the floor. Waheeda lit two torches that were clamped into brackets in the sides of the rock. The torches chased shadows from the room. The noise of the flicking flames added a soothing melody to the sound of the water from the underground river. After rolling some straw into a bundle, Waheeda placed it under her head and closed her eyes.

'Why didn't you tell me you were a girl?' Ali asked, stretching out on the floor and glancing over to her. Reflections of the candle flames danced off her golden hair. Her lips seemed to have been painted red by the flames and, even though her eyes were closed, he felt she was watching him.

'I was always me,' Waheeda muttered, without opening her eyes, 'you saw a boy.'

'You said your name was Waheed,' Ali protested.

'You heard what you heard.'

'But you were dressed as a boy.'

'Mmm,' Waheeda mumbled. 'Go to sleep.'

Ali rolled his own pillow and lay down.

Over the noise of the flowing of the river, he tried to work out where they were. The river flowed down towards the sea, therefore they had travelled south. How many miles had they travelled? Two, three, thirty? The boat had turned so many corners, he could not even be sure they had gone south. He concluded they must be in the marshlands which in ancient times, it was said, had hidden whole cities. An image of a city of flickering lights hidden amongst gently moving grass hovered in front of his eyes as he drifted into deep sleep.

Ali dreamed of fresh bread being baked. His mother brought him a large, steaming piece. He shoved it into his mouth but felt it sticking between his teeth. It was pricking into his flesh, embedding itself in his throat. He sat up, choking. Opening his eyes, he realised his mouth was full of straw. He was alone. The cave was full of light. He heard the river flowing and, behind it, muffled voices.

Brushing the straw off him, Ali walked into the main cave. Waheeda, her father, and the two men were sitting around a fire. Waheeda, with her back to them, beckoned to Ali to sit beside her. Ali nodded, but went in the opposite direction to wash himself in the cold waters of the river. When he returned, some fruit and bread were waiting for him on a cloth beside the fire. The two men were standing guard at the entrance.

'Eat. Eat. There is much to do,' said Waheeda's father.

Waheeda beamed a smile. Breaking a piece of bread, Ali looked her in the eyes until both of them broke their gaze in unspoken shyness. Waheeda had washed her face and her hair hung loose. He could definitely see a girl now, and felt embarrassed he hadn't noticed before.

'Are you sure he is the right person for the task, my child?' Waheeda's father whispered. His words only just reached Ali's ears above the sound of the river.

'He is strong for his size, father,' Waheeda answered, 'and what he lacks in wisdom he makes up for in courage.'

Waheeda's father ran his eyes over Ali who, pretending he had not heard, continued with his breakfast.

When Ali had finished his food, Waheeda's father stood up, towering over the other men. With his back to the light, he was a silhouette in front of Ali. 'Now, young man, it is time,' he announced.

'Time for what, sir?' Ali replied.

'Time for Waheeda and you to go out and destroy the evil that is attacking us,'

Ali and Waheeda remained quiet.

'The two of you must learn to watch the

wind and hear the silence. You must not fear the dark, but learn to hide in its crevices. Our enemy is powerful and cunning, but you are brave and have the power of youth. You must learn to strike at his very heart, but you must not take an innocent life.'

'But my sister was innocent,' Ali interrupted. 'The enemy did not care. We must talk to him in the language he will understand.'

Waheeda's father paused for a moment and said, 'You are right to be angry, my son. But anger alone is not enough. Anyone can shout. We have to destroy the enemy. And do not forget, we are all responsible for our actions or that which is done in our name. While you slept, I went to the well of ancient knowledge, and there I studied the hair which Waheeda brought. I learnt that, by the time the light of the next day comes, Khauf will be captured by King Gosler. He is going to be betrayed by one of his own. Now the long night of King Gosler's never-ending war has begun, and the world cannot know any peace until Gosler is dead. But King Gosler is not mortal. He keeps returning, decade after decade, in different guises. This is his darkest secret.' Waheeda's father turned to look at his daughter, then continued, 'King Gosler does not have a heart in his chest. His immortality is kept in his heart, and his heart is stored inside the body of a tiger that lives on the black mountain. You must find the tiger and destroy the heart. When this is done, King Gosler will become mortal and fear for his life. Prince Sticker will live as long as King Gosler lives, but he must forever live close to the king.'

One of the guards ran to Waheeda's father and whispered in his ear. The father nodded and continued, 'You have to succeed, only then will we regain our skies, our rivers, our seas and land, and our milk.'

'Where is the black mountain?' asked Ali.

'Go west and you will find it,' Waheeda's father replied. 'We must leave this place and go to the sanctuary of ancient treasures. We will be safe there. Gosler's soldiers are climbing the hill. They will be here very soon.'

'Surely they will follow us, father,' said Waheeda.

'You are but children,' said Waheeda's father, walking towards the opening of the cave. 'This land of ours is a cradle of all knowledge and civilisation. Over the last three thousand years, many invaders have come here. They have caused us immense pain, but none have ever touched the ancient treasures.'

'But King Gosler and Prince Sticker are

different,' Ali said. 'They are truly evil. I have seen them up close.'

'Do not question my wisdom!' Waheeda's father thundered. 'Now move!'

The Ancient City

Ali followed Waheeda and the three men out of the cave and into the light. They emerged onto a winding path through the hillside. As they climbed, they could see King Gosler's soldiers scaling the hillside, but the path reached a sharp incline and they stopped beside a twisted, dried out, river bed covered by overgrowth. They walked in the shade of the overgrowth while, overhead, strange fires streaked across the sky.

It was almost dark when they reached the ancient city. Avoiding the two guards who stood by the gates, they advanced into the courtyard and reached a blood red door. A thick beam inlaid with silver stars ran diagonally through its centre. Two panels,

each adorned with five silver stars, were
fitted into a frame carved with geometrical
shapes.   Ali could see no handle, but
Waheeda's father began to press the stars,

one after the other, then pressed two at the same time. The door opened inwards.

They found themselves in a room lit by the light of thousands of candles which illuminated the paintings that adorned the walls. Ancient pottery was stacked on shelves in a corner beside row upon row of books. Ali noticed an imposing stone carving of a bull. He remembered reading about this at school. It was said that this was the oldest carving in the whole world.

'This is just the first room,' Waheeda's father sighed. ' Ancient knowledge is buried in every brick in this building.'

Walking over to a cupboard, Waheeda's father pulled out a box. Blowing the dust off it, he said, 'I am going to give you three things. Use their power wisely.'

Waheeda's father placed three objects on a table before carefully closing the box and pushing it back.

Ali and Waheeda looked on as Waheeda's father unwrapped a small cloth sack. 'This cloak was made by the hands of a thousand tailors. Those who wear it become invisible to the eyes of their enemies. Visible to friends but invisible to foes. They become like a grain of sand in the desert, like a fish in the river. This sword will glow red when you are near the heart of Gosler,' he continued, as he pulled the shining blade out of its sheath. 'And this shield will repulse anything that is thrown at you.' Waheeda's father placed the shield and the cloak into a brown sack which he closed by pulling two cords. He placed the sword back in its sheath and left it on the table. Its strap quivered as it dangled off the edge.

Suddenly, one of the guards burst in, shouting, 'King Gosler and his men have surrounded us. They are demanding we hand them the secret camels.'

'We have no camels here,' Waheeda's father said.

'We told them, but they have given us one minute to hand over the camels or they will tear this place apart.'

'They will never do that,' Waheeda's father reassured them.

'I will stand and fight them,' said Ali.

'No, we must get away from here,' Waheeda implored. 'They will not stop.'

'All of humanity respects the sanctity of this place,' Waheeda's father protested.

'But you know they have no…'

Before Waheeda could finish her sentence, the door crashed to the ground.

'This way, Ali,' Waheeda shouted. 'I know a way out.'

Waheeda's father sat in the middle of the floor as a wall of ancient paintings was ripped apart. White light flooded in through the gaps. Waheeda rushed to her father, kissed his forehead, then picked up the sword and ran to an opening at the end of the room. Ali grabbed the sack with the shield and the cloak, strapped it around his back, and hurried to join her. Waheeda stopped and turned for a last glimpse of her father, as she hung the sword across her shoulders.

Two enormous dragon-like creatures, with big flat faces, were pulverising everything in front of them. They advanced towards the old man, who lowered his head in prayer.

'Father, stand up, please stand up,' Waheeda begged.

Lines of soldiers marched behind the monsters and fanned out around the room, grabbing what they could. There was the unmistakable smile of Prince Sticker, holding the leashes of Dir and Dur, while King Gosler followed, fast asleep on what looked like an elephant.

'Look how happy they are with their new master,' Waheeda remarked. The dogs' eyes flashed. Prince Sticker's smile widened. He unleashed the dogs.

'They've seen us,' Waheeda warned, pulling Ali through the opening. 'Move!'

Using all their strength, Waheeda and Ali pushed the stone door shut, just in time to keep out the dogs.

They were in a winding corridor with torches flickering at regular intervals, throwing huge shadows across the wall.

The steps as well as the walls and ceiling were carved out of solid rock. As Ali's eyes got accustomed to the light, he saw unlit torches in brackets alongside the burning ones. Waheeda took one and lit it.

'There are three hundred and thirty nine steps all together,' Waheeda informed him. 'They go all the way down to the well.'

'Is there a way out?'

'I have never been all the way down,' Waheeda replied, 'but father used to say there are secret passages inside the well.'

Ali and Waheeda began to descend the steps. The steps were uneven and they had to tread carefully. As they neared the well, Ali slipped and would have fallen had not Waheeda caught him. 'A rat,' she said, pointing to the dark shape hurrying away from them. Ali nodded, and continued his descent. Minutes later, they found themselves standing in the centre of an enormous cave, almost as big as the one they had just left. Each time they moved, their steps echoed against the wall. Ali noticed three other stairwells at opposite corners of the cave and, in the centre, the well. 'Best make sure we are safe,' Ali whispered.

The word 'safe' resounded throughout the cave, fading with each echo. Waheeda nodded, and Ali grabbed an unlit torch from the wall, lit it from Waheeda's, and walked around the well to check the other stairwells.

'Ali!' Waheeda screamed.

Her torch had fallen to the ground. Dark figures jumped from the shadows, pouncing on her.

'Ali, the sword!' Waheeda shouted, and tossed it towards him where it fell onto the edge of the well.

More figures were coming down the stairs

towards her. Dir and Dur's unmistakable barking began to resonate through the cave. Taking a deep breath, Ali dived into the well, deliberately knocking the sword in with his torch.

The torch hissed out of life as it hit the water. Catching the sword as it began to sink, Ali strapped it around his wrist. He could see a faint light at the bottom of the well which seemed to be coming from a small tunnel carved into its side. Ali swam down to it, and pulled himself along the flooded corridor until he saw another opening in the ceiling. A stinging breeze embraced him as he climbed through the hole. He was in a tunnel that veered upwards sharply. Exhausted, Ali began to crawl towards the exit.

By the time Ali reached the top, cold was ripping into his bones. Sweat dripped down his face while he shivered all over. Perhaps this is the day of judgement, he thought. Don't let me die here, Lord. My quest has just begun. 'Waheeda!' he called out.

As he emerged out of the tunnel, the wind wailed back. His head felt heavy. The darkness enveloped him. Strange faces, some elongated, others bloated, throbbed in front of him.

Ali slid down the hill, oblivious to the sharp stones or the thorns of wild bushes that ripped his skin. In the moonlight, he could see the silhouette of a house beyond some rocks and he began to drag himself towards it. Its broken door creaked as it swung to and fro and there was no ceiling. Ali crawled inside and rolled onto his back. All his strength left him.

On opening his eyes, Ali could see soft folds of green canvas above him. The howling of the wind had stopped and it was light outside. Ali was lying on his back in a tent, covered by a sheet. 'My sword,' he said in a panic. He tried to sit up, but slumped down again.

'We thieves respect each other,' said a familiar voice.

'Where are my things?' Ali asked, groping with his hand.

'Everything is safe. Do you not recognise your childhood friend, Hakim the wizard?'

'I recognise your voice, but please forgive me, I did not remember your name,' Ali apologised, and for the first time took a long hard look at this short chubby boy.

Hakim had only one foot. He still could not place him.

'Where are my things?' Ali repeated.

'We are honourable thieves, little brother,' Hakim assured him, limping from side to side. 'We do not steal from fellow thieves.'

'I am not a thief,' Ali protested, propping himself up. 'I have a mission.'

'Here you are,' Hakim said, passing the sack and sword to Ali.

Accepting Hakim's outstretched hand, Ali pulled himself up and asked, 'Are there more of you?'

'There's lots of room for another,' Hakim smiled. 'Especially one who is already armed.'

'I told you, I am not a thief.'

'No one is born a thief and no thief other than Hakim the wizard is proud of his art. I know no magic but I am still Hakim the wizard.'

As his eyes got more and more accustomed to the daylight, Ali began to realise how enormous the tent was. A number of beds were folded neatly along one side.

'This tent is our prize possession,' Hakim announced, rubbing his fat little hand through his unkempt hair. 'We took it from Gosler's soldiers.'

A fearful thought raced around Ali's head.

Placing his hands on his knees, Hakim bent double, laughing. 'You are scared of Hakim the little fat wizard?'

'I fear no one,' said Ali firmly.

'But we thieves are scared of everyone,' said Hakim, wiping his eyes.

'I am not a thief, nor do I wish to be one,' Ali remonstrated. 'But do tell me how you lost your foot.'

A sad twitch crossed Hakim's shining face. His eyes filled with tears. 'The miracle, younger brother, is that you have all your limbs.'

Ali knew he shouldn't have asked the question. He already knew the answer, having heard such stories many a time. Frustrated with Khauf, King Gosler had poisoned the land and air. Strange yellow bags had fallen from the skies. Wherever they landed, the earth became barren. The trees died. The wells dried. Migrating birds fell dead to the ground as they flew overhead and children were born with missing limbs. Some had their limbs fused together at birth. Many lost their mothers when they were born.

'I didn't mean to upset you, Hakim,' said Ali.

'I'd gone to the forest to collect firewood with my mother,' Hakim replied. 'There was a loud bang and I heard her calling me. I ran towards her, but there was a flash of light and I was thrown backwards. When I awoke I was in my uncle's house. My foot was missing.'

'And what of your mother?'

Hakim sighed. 'When you did not wake up on the seventh day, I thought you were on your way to meet your maker.'

Ali was aghast. 'I've been asleep for a week?'

'I thought you were off to eternal sleep. You kept saying, "I am so sorry for letting you down, Waheeda."'

Ali remembered. They had come out of the shadows. He tensed, 'They took Waheeda.'

'Now, Ali, son of Omani, we have all lost so much.'

'And my mother, she is alone now.' Ali lowered his eyes and wept.

Placing his hand on Ali's head, Hakim sat beside him in silence, while Ali dozed.

The darkness had fallen by the time Ali woke again. 'Come, it is time for food,' Hakim called from the entrance.

It was a cool, bright starry night. The air was full of the scent of roasting meat. A fire crackled close by and the sound of a flute floated in the air. The green canvas was invisible from outside. Flaming wild grass had locked itself into an arch that crossed from one end of a ridge to the other. The tent was pegged in the clearing underneath.

Ali followed Hakim over some wobbly rocks until they came onto a flat piece of earth. Four boys were sitting around a fire, the flute player leaning against the trunk of a tree. He nodded an acknowledgement to Ali and continued with his melody. A boy beside the flute player started to beat a rhythm on an overturned log and Hakim burst into a song:

You write Your God's name in the sand
And paint His image in the air
I am the grain you cannot see
I am the breath that will be free.

You write Your God's name in the sand
And sow the wind across our land
But I will never be forlorn
So reap the harvest of the storm

I wield the stick and lob the stone
And even with my shattered bone
I will rebuild my people's home.

Many more boys and girls came out of the hills while Hakim sang. When he had finished, they each shook Ali's hand. As he ate, Ali learned what had happened while he was unconscious.

King Gosler had taken over the country.

His soldiers were tearing everything apart in their search for flying camels. King Khauf had been captured and his army had fled. Many had joined Gosler. Long lines of soldiers were going westwards, taking as much milk and as much of everything else they could carry.

'Does anyone know anything about my mother, Fatima, the wife of Omani?' Ali asked.

No-one answered. After a while, Hakim replied, 'This is the secret hill of the orphans. Our land is our mother now. She is our beloved.'

'What do they do with those they capture?' Ali asked.

'The lucky ones are martyred. The others, if they are useful, are taken prisoner in Khauf's palace. Even the stone walls of the prison are shedding tears for them.' Hakim thought for a while, then raised his voice, addressing everyone. 'Brothers and sisters, this is our land. She is our mother. We are not orphans. Let us go to her. King Gosler is indeed powerful, but he cannot kill us all. He does not even know who we are.' Hakim picked up a fistful of earth, kissed it, and tossed it into the air. 'Let us, this night, vow to do whatever we have to do to lift our mother from under the feet of Gosler and his soldiers. This is the path of righteousness.'

The flute player stood and waved his flute through the air. It cried. Placing it back into his pocket, he said in an accent Ali had not heard before, 'My brothers and sisters, I have come to you from across the mountains, from the land of poets. Your evil king Khauf, at the behest of Gosler, forced an eight year war on all of us. We children will never fight each other. Just as my flute can play with the music of these hills, so can we, children of the two lands, join hands against Gosler's tyranny. God forbid, but if Gosler should win here, no one will be safe anywhere in the world. We will join you in setting the very earth on fire under the feet of Gosler's army. We children together can make him put his tail between his legs.'

The hill resounded to joyous shouting. After a few moments, the assembled boys and girls broke up into little groups and began to plan their attack.

'And what will you do?' Ali asked Hakim as he sat down.

Before he could answer, someone whistled. Hakim threw earth on the flames to extinguish the fire, and the boys and girls disappeared into the shadows of the hills as a loud whirring noise came towards them. Bushes swung violently, as though hit by a sudden storm. Ali closed his eyes against the grit and dust as a large dark object hovered over them. The noise was deafening.

Hakim shouted into Ali's ear: 'Don't move until it has gone.'

The monster began to fly away, beaming a bright light below. It was out of sight within moments, but Ali could still feel the wind. He looked around for the children. Only Hakim was there.

'What happened to the others?' Ali asked.

'We can disappear into the hills,' Hakim laughed, 'or merge into grains of sand or dissolve into water. Gosler's monsters will never catch us. You too can stay with us, if you wish.'

'You are truly generous, Hakim the wizard,' Ali smiled, embracing Hakim warmly. 'But I must go to the palace to look for Waheeda. Then I can finish my mission. If God wills it, I will be successful.'

'God is willing.' Hakim shook Ali's hand. 'Stay close to the hills.'

Strapping the sword around his shoulders, Ali clasped Hakim's hands in his. Winking at him, he tied the cords of the sack around his head and turned away.

The night had deepened. The air was

filled with the song of crickets. Moonlight rained down on the hills, throwing protective shadows in Ali's path. Owls, foxes, jackals and other creatures of the night called out in protection as dried branches crushed under his feet. How wondrous the hills were, he thought. In the daylight, when the sun was fierce, they were dry and brown, yet how different those same colours looked now, in the moonlight.

Ali walked for most of the night along a track high in the hills. At times he could see the ancient river in the distance, shining like a silvery snake. As dawn was breaking he reached the top of the last hill, from where he would be able to see the palace. But when he looked down, what he saw he could not have imagined in his wildest nightmares.

Ali could see the entire city. Many buildings were on fire. The outer walls of Khauf's palace were broken and much of the interior was reduced to smouldering ruins. Strange objects slithered across the skyline leaving thin white streaks as if drawing lines with the clouds. Long rows of people, some in carts, others on foot, were streaming out of the city, going past the palace and towards the desert.

Ali took off his sword, put the sack down and stretched out on the ground. He stared at an ant that was carrying a leaf much bigger than itself. He placed a few small rocks in the path of the ant. Each time it got stuck, it moved around the obstacle and continued on its journey.

Opening his sack, Ali pulled out the cloak. It looked different from when he had seen it last. The patches appeared larger and the cloth seemed more worn. It felt heavier too. Ali put the sword around his shoulders, the sack's cord over his head, and slipped into the cloak. He looked up and down his arm. He could still see it. Then he remembered Waheeda's father's words: 'Visible to friends, invisible to foes.'

Walking towards a line of people, Ali froze in terror as a heavy voice boomed out over and over again: 'Bring us the head of Ali, son of Omani, and you will be richly rewarded.'

Strangely dressed soldiers looked menacingly over the mass of moving humanity. One of the soldiers shouted at Ali then began to walk towards him. Ali grabbed the handle of his sword. A masked man walking next to the soldier pointed to the line of people and thundered, 'Get back in line, over there with the rest of the rubbish.'

'They can't distinguish me from anyone else,' thought Ali, smiling to himself.

Lowering his head, Ali walked into the throng of people. They were being herded towards a field close to Khauf's palace where people stood silently, waiting for something to happen. Eventually King Gosler and Prince Sticker emerged from the palace. King Gosler was picking morsels from his teeth, but Prince Sticker's teeth glistened as he strolled out with Dir and Dur on either side of him.

King Gosler was wearing a tall hat, with shining tassels dangling from its rim. His skin-tight trousers ripped as he climbed a large statue of Khauf. The statue was the pride and joy of King Khauf, the biggest one he had ever had made. The hand of the statue was where he used to stand and watch his soldiers march past. King Gosler climbed to the very top of the statue and slid joyfully down Khauf's nose, along an outstretched arm, and hopped off onto the hand. He stood up and let out a loud exaggerated belch and said, 'Horrible, horribilists. Ali. Bloody devil's blood.'

Prince Sticker was dressed in the same black cloak in which Ali had last seen him. Today, however, he wore a bright blue shirt. He tied the dogs to the base of the statue and climbed up next to King Gosler.

Prince Sticker spoke slowly: 'Good people of this bountiful land, King Gosler has finally come to you at the calling of the Court of Peace. We have delivered you from the evil tyranny of Khauf. You do not have to fear him or his secret camels any more. If you have any information about these secret camels, then speak to us. You

will be richly rewarded. There are those among you who would like to stamp out this march of freedom. They are your enemy. Your country has become a magnet for all manner of these people. There is one among them who is the embodiment of evil itself. His life's mission is to kill our beloved King Gosler. The name of this terrible creature is Ali. He is a clever little boy who can speak just like you, but make no mistake, he has the blood of the devil in his veins. Anyone giving us information about him will be richly rewarded.'

A few soldiers clapped enthusiastically while everyone else remained solemnly still. Throughout Sticker's speech, King Gosler continued to pick his teeth, wiping his spit on the sides of his arms. Apart from the occasional barking of the dogs, no-one else made a sound. When he had finished, the soldiers climbed on top of each other, creating human steps. King Gosler and Prince Sticker waved benignly to the assembled crowd, then climbed down over the soldiers.

Ali went unnoticed to one side and edged his way to the front. Prince Sticker untied the dogs and waited for King Gosler, who kept waving his hand. Ali unsheathed his sword and shield and inched away from the crowd. The dogs, with eyes raging, turned towards him.

Prince Sticker looked in the direction where the dogs were pulling. Reining them in, he ordered, 'Stop barking at shadows'.

Ali waited for King Gosler's entourage to pass and, slipping by the snapping dogs, wove his way past the guards and entered the palace. The ground was littered with debris, but the main residence had survived undamaged. King Gosler and Prince Sticker entered the residence. Four huge soldiers with masked faces stood motionless in front of a door. Ali waited, took a deep breath, and stepped forward. One of the soldiers shouted, 'Who goes there?'

Ali stopped in his tracks. The other soldiers tensed and laughed, shaking their heads in disbelief at their colleague. The soldier who had shouted lifted his helmet. His face was ghostly white with terrified blue eyes. Stepping apprehensively towards Ali, he said, 'I saw someone there by the door.'

'Oh, you saw the ghost of a shadow,' one of the soldiers replied over the laughter of his colleagues. 'Who would dare to come here?'

Holding on to his sword, Ali backed away. As the soldier inched fearfully forward, Ali edged behind him. The red neck of the soldier was exposed. Ali steadied his hand, took aim with his sword, then, changing his mind, kicked the soldier on the bum. The soldier stumbled and fell, much to the amusement of his colleagues.

Placing his sword back in its sheath, Ali slipped past the guards and entered Khauf's residence. He was in a massive room. A huge sparkling chandelier dangled from the central dome of the ceiling. King Gosler was alone and admiring himself in a mirror that hung from the wall. He was wearing only a pair of thin shorts. Though he had no biceps to speak of, he was nevertheless flexing them in front of the mirror and straightening his chest. Ali couldn't help laughing at the antics of King Gosler.

'Who what where is which?' King Gosler asked fearfully, staring at the long silk curtain that hung from the ceiling.

'You, the most powerful king on earth, are scared of Ali,' said Ali, clenching the sword tightly.

King Gosler ran to the furthest corner, staring at shadows and screaming, 'Damn country. Damn, damn, doodles.'

'Where is Waheeda?' Ali demanded. 'Tell me now or I will cut out your heart.'

At the mention of the word 'heart', King Gosler began to laugh, and Ali remembered the advice of Waheeda's father. King Gosler had no heart in his body. His heart was kept inside a tiger.

The door opened and Prince Sticker

entered. He flung a dressing gown at King Gosler and turned to leave before saying, 'The staff are waiting.'

Looking around nervously, King Gosler threw the gown around himself and ran out of the room. Ali followed him, keeping at a safe distance.

Several generals were sitting around a large table. Prince Sticker was marching back and forth, lost in thought. King Gosler jumped onto the table on all fours, arching his back and screeching, 'Talking rooms. Camels. Flying camels. Happy, happy people. Milky silky kilky milk.'

Prince Sticker, eternally smiling, translated the King's words: 'His Majesty wants you to tear this land to pieces and find him those camels. He says you have done a wonderful job in making the people of this country free and happy.' Sitting in a chair at the top of the table, Prince Sticker ordered: 'Now go, and make sure every last drop of milk is loaded and removed from this place.'

The generals stood, bowed and left. Ali moved into a corner.

King Gosler jumped up and clapped his hands. A moment later a guard entered, leading a shackled man. Ali recognised Waheeda's father at once. King Gosler clapped his hands again and the guard forced the prisoner to stand straight. As King Gosler hopped around the table, crowing, Prince Sticker said, 'Now, old man, the only way you can save your daughter's life is to tell us where Ali is.'

'The secret of your mortality is no more,' said Waheeda's father.

'We know from our spies that you have confided in a puny little boy called Ali,' Prince Sticker boasted. 'And we know you have sent him west, back to our kingdom and the black mountain.' Prince Sticker laughed. 'You idiotic old man. We are not stupid enough to leave our mortality behind. It is at our rear camp, guarded by the best in our mighty army.'

Waheeda's father turned his head towards Ali and said heavily, 'People like you would not be able to see your destroyer if he was standing next to you.'

Prince Sticker thundered, 'Take this man out of here! Make him talk!'

Maintaining a safe distance from the guard, Ali followed as Waheeda's father was led down long winding corridors. The sound of people weeping resonated all around him, growing louder the further he went into the palace. Every now and then a sharp painful scream would echo down the corridor. Waheeda's father was frog-marched into a large prison wing connected to Khauf's main residence.

'How long are you going to keep my daughter in cell 666?' Waheeda's father said, as loudly as his frail voice could manage.

The soldier kicked Waheeda's father, who stumbled and fell. He hissed, 'Why are you talking to shadows, you stupid old man?'

As he was pushed into a cell, the old man stole a glance at Ali and smiled. Ali smiled back. The cell was at the beginning of a long winding corridor full of identical cells. As Ali made his way down the corridor, he heard strange music. It was more of a screeching rhythm than anything he would call music, and coming from the end of the corridor. As he made his way towards the source of the sound, the corridor opened into a hall from which ran numerous other corridors.

Some of the guards were dancing, others were drinking. Almost everyone Ali looked at seemed to be in a drunken stupor.

Ali turned to enter the corridor for cell 666 and stood horrified.

The Pyramid

Men and women, injured and groaning, were piled on top of one another in a heap in front of cell 666. Two soldiers, a man and a woman, danced around the human pile, embracing each other. A third soldier sat on a large chair, carefully drawing the scenery.

Cell 666 was a long thin room. Ali saw Waheeda curled up in a corner, her head lowered over her knees.

Ali tapped gently on the bars of her cell and Waheeda looked up in astonishment.

'Ali,' Waheeda whispered, 'you must leave now. They must not catch you.'

'They can't catch what they cannot see,' Ali replied.

Waheeda crawled towards the front and

asked softly, 'My father…have you seen my father?'

'He is well,' Ali said, hesitating.

'I knew you would come.'

'I need you with me,' Ali replied.

'All the gates of all the cages will be opened at the same time, after those two have finished dancing. They will search through the pile of poor souls and those who have died will be thrown onto a cart and taken away. My best chance of escape is to be thrown onto the cart.'

'I will distract them when the doors open. You go to the pile.'

The music began to fade. 'It is time,' Waheeda warned.

The gates of the cells opened with a sharp, clanging noise. As it subsided, Ali withdrew his sword and rattled the bars of the cell. The soldiers started in surprise and Ali ran behind them and struck one

with his sword; it did not pierce the soldier's armour, but he yelled in shock and others ran to his assistance. As Ali sneaked closer to the pile, Waheeda slipped out of the cell.

A soldier pulled prisoners out of the pile and flung them onto the cart. Ali threw his cloak around Waheeda and both of them climbed onto the cart as it began to move. They were close to the exit when they heard the dogs.

The barking of Dir and Dur filled the air. Ali saw Prince Sticker entering from the opposite end, straining to hold the dogs. Tall metal bars divided the hall into two. The dogs were on the other side.

A guard looked over the cart, opened the gate, and slammed it shut immediately after the cart had left.

Prince Sticker, unable to hold the dogs, unleashed them. The beasts charged down the hall as terrified soldiers jumped out of their way.

On seeing the raging beasts, the soldier guarding the outer exit jumped up, grabbed a pole, and perched on top of the gate.

The dogs, frustrated at their path being blocked, tried to bite their way to the other

side. Prince Sticker shouted a command. A soldier opened the gate and the dogs sniffed the ground and charged out.

By the time the dogs were outside, Ali and Waheeda had left the cart and were running towards the outer wall of the palace. Prince Sticker and his soldiers, raced after the dogs. People were screaming and running helter-skelter.

Slipping out of the cloak, Waheeda and Ali ran as fast as their legs would carry them.

They came out of the palace at the opposite end from the river, where the land fell into a deep gorge. 'We can only go as far as that bush,' panted Ali.

'Keep going, we can outdo those dumb dogs,' Waheeda replied.

The Search Begins

Although the dogs' barking was faint, it was getting closer.

'Do you remember the story of the Lion and the Rabbit?' Ali asked Waheeda.

'Yes, the lion jumps at its own reflection,' Waheeda replied.

They moved gingerly to the edge of the gorge and looked down. It was so deep they could see nothing at the bottom. Leaning over, they noticed a small ledge, big enough for both of them to sit on. A bush twisted from the sides of the gorge and bent skywards. The dogs' barking got nearer.

'This will do,' Ali said, pointing to the overhanging branches.

'Perfect,' agreed Waheeda.

Tying a piece of cloth around the shield, Ali said, 'You go down and hold the cloth, I will lure the dogs.'

'No, I'll do that. You go down,' Waheeda protested.

'We only have moments,' Ali shouted. 'Go!'

Waheeda climbed onto the ledge, placed the shield inside the branches and held the cloth. The shield shone like a mirror in the brilliant sunshine.

'They've seen me.' Ali shouted, running towards the ledge. 'Come on, you monsters!' Ali taunted, jumping onto the ledge beside Waheeda.

The dogs stopped on top of them. Their saliva dribbled into the gorge below. Seeing their own reflections in the shield, the dogs became more and more angry. When they opened their mouths, the dogs in the shield opened theirs too. As they

flashed their bloodshot eyes, so did the dogs in the shield. But it was the barking back of the dogs below that really enraged Dir and Dur. It echoed back out of the gorge. They jumped. As they did this, Waheeda pulled the shield away, and the dogs crashed through the twigs and fell yelping into the gorge, becoming two tiny dots before they disappeared.

'The world will be a safer place without

those two, who couldn't even be faithful to their own master,' said Waheeda, as she pulled the shield back onto the ledge.

They heard Prince Sticker, accompanied by soldiers, standing above them, calling out to the dogs. Waheeda and Ali held their breath as they sat on the ledge, their backs pressed against the cliff-side, hidden by the overhanging branches.

Ali Talks to the Camel

After calling the dogs until he was hoarse, Prince Sticker cursed them and returned to the palace. The soldiers followed him.

When she was certain the soldiers had gone, Waheeda whispered to Ali, 'It should be safe now.'

Ali did not reply.

Looking out at the vast expanse of the gorge, Waheeda sat back, letting out a deep sigh. Even though she was sitting on the edge of the precipice, the sight was truly magnificent. Flocks of migrating birds flew by in tight formations, gliding through little puffs of clouds. The wind, brushing against the sides of the rocks, whistled an enchanting melody. The mighty fireball of

the sky was beyond the other side of the
gorge that seemed to be painted with rising
crimson streaks. Waheeda closed her
eyes, soaking it in, until a strange humming
sound ripped through the music of the

wind. Opening her eyes, Waheeda saw the flocks of birds breaking formation. Something long and thin with narrow blue flames was cutting through the birds.

'Ali, look,' Waheeda prodded Ali. 'The sun has set.'

Waheeda kept her eyes on the blue flames as they raced through the expanse. The gorge burst with a loud bang, like a thousand cracks of lightning. All manner of petrified birds began to fly out of the sides.

'We must fear nothing,' Ali declared, climbing over the ridge. 'We have to find the heart. God willing, we will end this nightmare.'

Ali offered his hand to Waheeda. Pulling herself up she replied, 'God is willing,'

Beyond the shattered walls in front of them stood the broken buildings of the palace. The palace was built in between the river and the gorge. Ali and Waheeda made their way cautiously along the outer wall towards the other side of the palace.

Outside the palace, people were camped on both banks of the river. The cries of sleepless children filled the air. A woman was cooking in a large earthen pot that stood inside a fire. She saw the hungry looks on the faces of Ali and Waheeda and said, 'Come children, come eat.'

Ali's mouth watered, but he saw her children sitting patiently, huddled together. 'God bless you aunty, but we have just eaten,' he lied.

The old woman broke a piece of bread and, handing it to Ali, said, 'Take this, my son, for when you are hungry next. We have more food than we need.'

'We have to eat,' Waheeda whispered.

Lowering his head, Ali accepted the bread and, bidding farewell to the old lady, they continued on their way. They had hardly finished eating when an old man came to them. He was holding two glasses in his hands. 'Drink this, my children,' he said. 'I will not let my milk be taken by those thieves who destroyed our homes.'

'We need to find a way of getting to the western borders,' Ali told the old man after drinking the milk. 'Where can we find transport for this journey?'

'The wealthy, they are all leaving,' the old man replied.

'We have no wealth, sir,' Ali replied. 'We only have a quest.'

The old man thought for a while and then replied, 'Where you wish to go can only be reached on a ship of the desert. Go down to the first bend in the river. Turn left at the bottom, and there you will find the house of Hussain. It is hidden from view. He will help you. Tell him Dahal sent you.'

The Ship of the Desert

The house was indeed hidden from view. As far as the eye could see there were only stumps of smouldering trees. Flames flickered a few yards away from Ali and Waheeda.

Hussain was an old man, much older than Dahal. He sat on the stump of an old tree with his feet on top of a pile of ropes and blankets, looking past the flames and into the flowing waters of the river.

'I have one left,' said Hussain, without waiting for the question. 'When he was born he was wild, and has been ever since. Go straight into the desert. He is a brave, if careless, beast. He will find you.'

'We have a long journey to make. Could you give us something in which we can take fresh water? We will pay you when we return,' Ali promised.

Putting his hand to his side, Hussain pulled out a shining black goatskin. Throwing it towards Ali he said, 'What use is money now?'

Catching the goat skin, Ali went to the well which was covered by a frame made from logs. Tied to the frame was a rope from which dangled an open-mouthed leather sack. Ali passed the goatskin to Waheeda, untied the rope, and dropped the sack into the well, pulling it up after a few seconds when it had filled with water. Waheeda filled the goatskin from the sack and, after drawing another load of water, each took turns to wash their hands and faces before drinking their fill. As they were turning to leave, Hussain said, 'Young blood is always eager to flow.'

'Have we done something to offend you,

sir?' Ali asked, looking at Waheeda in bewilderment.

'How will you sit on the camel?' said Hussain, stepping off the pile of ropes and pulling out a saddle and a tasselled blanket from underneath it.

Ali was about to lift the saddle and blankets onto his head when Hussain flicked his busy eyebrows at Waheeda and said, 'It will be easier if you hold one end each.'

Doing as he suggested, Ali and Waheeda realised at once that the saddle was much too heavy for one person to lift. They bade farewell to Hussain and left, hoping they would find the camel soon.

As they walked, the song of the flowing waters of the river began to fade until it became a memory. They began to walk more slowly, hampered by the weight of the saddle, until they reached an endless expanse of sand dunes. As they stopped in exhaustion, one of the dunes began to move.

'That must be him,' Ali whispered.

It took a few moments for them to focus their eyes and see it clearly. The camel was shaking its head and had turned his long neck towards them. Froth dribbled from his mouth. He blinked sadly with his large eyes before bending onto his front legs and sitting down with a thud.

'It's as though he knew we were coming,' Ali mused, walking towards the camel.

Running her hand over the camel's neck and over its hump, Waheeda answered, 'Look at the sorrow in his eyes. He too has seen what is happening.' The camel's hump trembled.

Ali unwrapped the saddle. It consisted of two heavily padded planks attached to two pairs of forked logs with a cushioned seat on top. Panting, Ali and Waheeda lifted it onto the camel and fastened it in place with four leather straps, spreading the blanket neatly over the sides. Ali sat in front, holding onto the reins, the sword and shield dangling off his back. While Ali climbed up, Waheeda secured the goatskin to the side of the saddle, then climbed behind him, leaning against the backrest.

'Ship of the desert, take us west, as far and as fast as you can go,' said Ali.

'He's just a camel,' said Waheeda.

The camel sniffled and Ali said, 'Hushu-Hushu, take us to the base camp of King Gosler's army.'

The camel stood with a few awkward jerks and set off westward. Waheeda leaned forward and rested her head on Ali's shoulder, rocking in the saddle as if floating over rough seas.

They went deeper and deeper into the

desert. Ali stared at the sandy world bathed in the bright golden moonlight, and suddenly the camel tensed. A chill wind dug into them. In front of them, a dark shadow was approaching.

'Oh God, it's cold,' Waheeda shivered.

'A storm is coming.' Ali shouted, covering his eyes against the stinging sand that smashed into his face. 'Hold on tight. We

have to get out of this fast!'

The camel quickened to a trot and raced forward into a reddish brown cloud. Waheeda buried her face into Ali's shoulder while Ali wrapped a piece of cloth over his eyes. The deeper they advanced, the more intense the storm became. Ali pulled on the reins, shouting, 'Hushu-Hushu.'

The camel stopped but would not sit down. Ali again commanded him to sit down. As Ali loosened the reins, the camel slumped to the ground, letting out a guttural moan.

Ali and Waheeda crawled beside the camel and huddled together, tucking a blanket beneath them as it fluttered furiously in the raging storm.

'I thought I heard someone wailing,' said Ali.

'In all this madness?' Waheeda replied.

Slowly, the howling wind ebbed away and the storm lost its anger. All of a sudden, everything went silent. The dark cloud had disappeared and the world was once again drenched in moonlight. Ali and Waheeda stood up, brushing sand from their clothes. The camel purred, turning its neck towards them, its third eyelid moving from side to side.

After checking his sword, shield and cloak, Ali began clambering up the nearest dune. Waheeda walked around the back of the camel and shouted, 'We have lost our water.'

Ali adjusted his shield and sword and continued to climb. The slope was very sharp and he had to dig his feet into the sand to stop himself falling backwards.

'We are not going to last without water,' Waheeda shouted, as Ali reached the top.

Ali did not reply. He was staring in horror

at the plumes of smoke rising out of the ruins of a small hamlet of houses. The faint sound of someone crying drifted over the gentle breeze which brushed through his dusty hair. Something flashed amidst the smoke and a bright red beam of light touched the ground close to his feet. He heard a deafening sound. Then he was tossed into the air.

'Ali, are you OK?' asked Waheeda.

'I am well, thank God,' Ali replied, recovering his breath. He noticed two figures running towards him. Another was moving in a circular movement towards the end of the long dune on which Ali was standing. Ali began to crawl, adding quickly, 'Grab the reins of the camel.'

'It is too late,' Waheeda replied. 'He has run away.'

'King Gosler's soldiers have found us,' Ali whispered.

'Give me the sword,' Waheeda whispered, holding out her hand. 'Use the shield.'

Ali tossed the sword and the cloak to Waheeda. She caught them, wrapped the cloak around her shoulders, drew the sword, and ran along the base of the dune.

Two red lights were scouring the ground near Ali. Each time the lights stopped there was a loud bang followed by a cloud of smoke and dust. Raising his shield, Ali stood and faced the approaching soldiers who aimed at him with their weapons. Two red dots flashed on the shield. Ali steadied himself, and moments later the ground under the soldiers exploded. Ali looked to his right. The third soldier was slumped over and Waheeda, who was walking away from him, slumped to her knees, the sword in her hand falling to the ground. 'Waheeda!' Ali screamed, running towards her.

Waheeda lifted her head as Ali drew near. Tears streamed down her cheeks. She raised the sword. It was covered with stick, blood-stained sand.

'We did what had to be done,' Ali said, trying to comfort her.

Waheeda said nothing, but looked up at the sky. Following her gaze, Ali noticed the first rays of sun, announcing the coming of a new dawn. It brought with it an anguished wail.

The Heart

'Did you hear that?' Ali asked pointing to the wind. 'Someone is crying.'

'The desert plays tricks,' said Waheeda solemnly.

The sound came again and this time it was unmistakable. A grief-filled cry, that cut through the night, was coming from the ruins of the hamlet.

Ali took the sword from Waheeda, wiped it clean on the sand, placed it back in the sheath and swung it around his shoulders.

'We must not be deflected from our mission,' Ali said, answering the look in Waheeda's eye.

'Someone may need our help,' Waheeda replied, walking towards the ruins.

'We have no time to waste.'

Waheeda ignored him and continued on.

'You either turn around now, or I will go on my own.'

Waheeda did not turn. The wailing had become a sob.

Ali stood motionless, then ran after Waheeda.

'I knew you would come,' Waheeda smiled.

Ali drew his sword. 'It may be a trap.'

'Look!' said Waheeda, sorrowfully pointing to the centre of the ruins.

Ali followed her gaze. A broken wall ran around the ruins of twelve houses which were built around a square. Inside the square was a boy about the same age as Ali, standing beside a donkey. The boy's head was lowered.

Ali and Waheeda walked up to the boy, smiling reassuringly. Without looking at them, the boy began to speak.

'I went to collect water as I do every day. It is hard to find water now. The foreign soldiers have taken over all the wells. Every night I go with my donkey while it is dark and return just before dawn. I used to get water from the Oasis of the Farms, but now it too has been taken over. I went last night to the hills beyond the oasis and collected the water from the fountain of the black rock. They were all here when I left. Now I am all that is left.'

The boy's thick, curly hair was covered in dust which fell onto his shoulders as he talked. His face was zigzagged with cuts and bruises, and his clothes torn in many places. He stood barefoot on the debris of the houses.

'God is with us,' Waheeda comforted. 'We are not alone.'

The boy raised his head. He looked first at Waheeda with his black bloodshot eyes, and then at Ali. 'Why are you coming in this direction when the world flees the opposite way?'

'We are after the heart of King Gosler,' Ali replied.

'It will be in his chest,' the boy sniggered, 'but they are hiding something very important in a big square room they have built on the hill above the farms. It is guarded by giant soldiers who only eat for an hour then sleep for an hour. I have watched them often and taken water from under their noses. They are so sure of their strength and the terror it inspires that they do not believe anyone will come this way.' The boy stopped mid-sentence, walked to the side of the donkey, picked up a stick, and stuck it into the ground. Pointing to the shadow, he continued, 'It is a two hour walk in that direction. When you get to the valley of the trees, you will find the giant soldiers.

If you want to get past them, wait until they have eaten.' The boy put his hand to one side of the donkey, pulled out a goatskin, and offered it to Ali, saying, 'You need to drink.'

'Come with us,' Ali said, accepting the water gratefully.

'I have found no bodies,' the boy said, climbing onto the back of the donkey. Maybe they have been taken away from here.' And the boy pressed his heels gently into the donkey and set off in the direction from which Ali and Waheeda had come.

Ali and Waheeda drank some water before continuing on their quest.

'How beautiful this dawn wind is,' Waheeda whispered, after they crossed the outer wall. Pointing to a small bush, she added, 'Even here the umbrella tree has managed to take root.'

Ali held the shield above his head, to

protect them from the sun. They were hungry and the heat was oppressive.

'How far do you think we have to go?' asked Waheeda. 'We must rest first.'

'Listen!' Ali said, taking her arm and stopping.

The muzzled sound of men singing floated in over the rising heat.

'I heard this song in prison,' said Waheeda, recognising the rhythm.

Ali felt a rush of energy race through his body. Hiding under the cloak, he and Waheeda made their way towards the singing. Ahead of them the ground dipped into a valley lined with row upon row of trees. Behind the trees rose an enormous grey building on a square plateau.

Ali and Waheeda slipped quietly into the welcome shade of the trees and made their way towards the square building.

The singing stopped. The air was full of

the sound of laughter and the din of loud chatter. Ali and Waheeda inched forward until they saw them.

These were the tallest men they had ever seen, as tall as the tallest camel. Their chests were as wide as those of a mountain bear and looked all the bigger because of their armour. They all had short blond hair, fat hairy noses, and open mouths from which stuck yellowing teeth. Many soldiers were sitting around a table grabbing roasted chickens that were piled high in the centre. Beside them, a cow was roasting on a spit. Some of the soldiers were trying to push whole chickens into their mouths while others tore flesh from the cooked cow with their teeth. Ali and Waheeda waited for the soldiers to eat their fill. As the boy on the donkey had said, eventually, one by one, the soldiers began to doze off. Some of them did this after

burping loudly, others after letting out the longest of farts imaginable, while others stretched their arms and yawned before dropping their faces into plates of food. All of them snored so loudly it made the trees shake.

Waheeda and Ali covered themselves with the cloak as they made their way towards the square room, stepping around the sleeping soldiers. The smell of their breath was so bad that they had to hold their noses. As they got closer to the square building they could see that it was made out of tree trunks and a soldier was fast asleep in front of the door, his great big hand resting on the padlock. Intermittently, Waheeda and Ali heard the roar of a tiger.

Suddenly, the ground began to vibrate.

They were about to move when they heard a loud noise as if a herd of elephants was charging towards them. Ali ran out from the cloak to get a better view. Small dots were running in front of what looked like a massive dust storm. Someone grabbed Ali's arm. He froze.

'You must hurry,' gasped the boy they had seen earlier, jumping off his donkey. 'King Gosler and Prince Sticker are on their way here.' The boy shook Ali's hand before mounting the donkey and adding, 'I will try to slow them down.'

Stepping closer to the door, Ali lifted the soldier's hand from the handle. The soldier let out a long whistling snore, yawned, and swung his other arm backwards. Ali dived and only just managed to get out of the way as Waheeda held back a snigger. Ali drew his sword and was about to strike the soldier when Waheeda shook her head. She bent to the ground and picked up a small twig and tickled the soldier's ear. The soldier muttered something, opened his mouth and smiled. Bits of chicken were stuck in the gaps between his teeth. Ali put the end of the sword into the lock and waited while Waheeda stuck the twig up the soldier's nose. The soldier sat up, sneezing loudly. Bits of food, spit and snot shot passed Waheeda. As the soldier sneezed Ali yanked the lock and both he and Waheed rushed in, slamming the door shut after them. They could hear the soldier shouting at his sleeping companions.

Waheeda bolted the door from the inside.

The two of them stood transfixed at the site in front of them. A tiger, with blue eyes, a white body and red stripes, stood in the centre of the room, its mouth wide open as if roaring, but there was no sound. Its eyes glittered like stars.

Above the tiger dangled a rectangular cage. The bars were made of horizontal and diagonal rods. Light shone down from

an opening in the ceiling. Perched inside the cage, its head drooping sadly, was a white dove.

Beneath the cage, a small fat man, naked from the waist upwards, crawled backwards in terror.

'The tiger is not moving,' Ali said in amazement.

'How can it?' the fat man replied, trembling. 'It is made of paper.'

The room began to shake with the approaching of Gosler's army. Something sharp hit the wall. Ali guessed it to be an axe. He moved closer to the fat man.

'Then how did it roar?' asked Waheeda.

'That was me,' the fat man replied dejectedly. 'That is all I ever do, roar like a tiger. And how I hate it. Oh, how I hate it.'

The sword was glowing red, but as Ali approached the tiger the glow diminished.

'There is no heart in this paper tiger,' Waheeda said, kicking it. Her foot ripped through it.

Ali turned his sword towards the fat man. The glow became even fainter.

'Tell me where the heart is or this is your last day on earth,' Ali threatened, raising the sword above his head. As he did so, the sword began to glow brighter. More and more blows landed against the wall outside, and some of the logs began to splinter.

'Open this door at once,' Prince Sticker thundered, banging on the door.

'It is in the dove,' Waheeda shouted, pointing above his head.

With a quick movement of his sword, Ali cut through the bars of the cage. The dove fell to the ground. The heart was stuck under its feathers. As Ali's sword touched the heart it fell throbbing to the ground - a thick slimy sludge.

The dove lifted its head, looking at Ali with gratitude.

'Open this door,' pleaded Prince Sticker. 'You can have anything you want but please, please, spare the heart.'

'Withdraw your soldiers,' Ali ordered. 'And

leave our land.'

'As you wish, but spare the heart,' said Prince Sticker.

The blows against the wall stopped.

Ali stuck the sword into the heart and lifted it into the air. He heard King Gosler mumbling fearfully outside. Waheeda grabbed the paper tiger and unlocked the door. Ali kicked it open and stepped outside, holding the heart at the end of his sword. King Gosler and Prince Sticker stepped back in terror as Waheeda emerged with the paper tiger. Even the giant soldiers gasped. Waheeda threw the paper tiger into the fire. King Gosler fell to his knees, 'We will make you king of this land,' Prince Sticker cried, 'but please spare the heart.'

Ignoring Prince Sticker, Ali threw the heart into the air. Prince Sticker and King Gosler ran frantically towards it as Ali sliced it into pieces. Waheeda shouted with joy.

Relieved of its burden, the dove circled Ali's head for a moment and then flew up into the sky.

Gosler started neighing, while Sticker wept, 'Save your life, Gosler, we are doomed!'

Gosler and Sticker, followed by the soldiers, ran for their lives. People chased them from every direction, throwing anything they could find at them. Even birds started to poo on the fleeing army. Gosler and Sticker ran and ran and ran and as far as I know they are still running today, plotting their return.

A New World

The beggar stopped his tale and ran his eyes over the spellbound audience.

The dove in the banyan tree had stopped singing and a few drops of rain began to pepper the tree as the ground let out a deep earthy scent. A cool wind rustled through the leaves and roots swayed joyously.

'Now, if you would be so kind as to let me end this tale, I may drink some water,' the beggar said.

'But old man, take off your hood so we may see your face,' said the woman, whose child had fallen asleep.

'Do not ask this of me,' the beggar replied. 'I wish to leave you with but a pleasant memory of a story told by a faceless stranger.'

'Did Ali find his father?' someone asked.

'Ali did find his mother,' the beggar replied. 'She was in the front of the crowd that came to greet them on their return home. Ali was about to cry when his mother looked over to Waheeda and asked, 'Have you come back to me on your wedding day?' And Ali blushed.'

'Waheeda's father also stood in the crowd and Waheeda ran and embraced him. Hakim was by his side holding a rope tied around the neck of Khauf. Addressing the crowd, Waheeda's father said, 'I know all of you want revenge on Khauf for what he has done. But I say enough of the bloodshed. We have all stood up. There will never be another Khauf. We must let him live and, like everyone else, make him work for a living. From this day forward, he will never accept anything for free. Not even a drop of

water.'

The beggar leaned forward, picked up the bowl of water, turned his head away from his audience and quenched his thirst. After placing the empty bowl inside his cloak, he grabbed his staff and walked around the back of the banyan tree.

The woman did not move. A tear rolled down her cheek. Her son, along with the other the children, got up to follow the beggar. But he was nowhere to be seen.

Also by Satchel

The Singer and the Snorer, *Peter Kalu*
Anansi The Spider and Tiger's Stew, *Peter Kalu*
Half Brother/Pahi Adha, *Tariq Mehmood*

www.satchel.info